Peter's Railway
Rain, Steam and Speed

by
Christopher Vine

The watercolour illustrations are by John Wardle

Published by
Christopher Vine 2016

Printed by The Amadeus Press
Copyright © 2016 Christopher Vine

ISBN 978-1-9088970-77

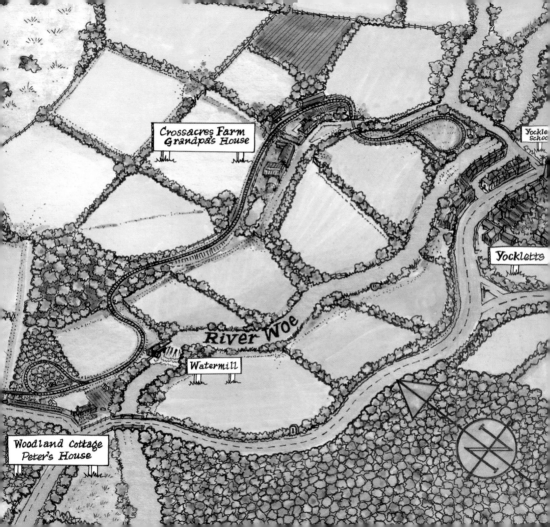

Crossacres Farm
Grandpa's House

Yockle
School

Yockletts

River Woe

Watermill

Woodland Cottage
Peter's House

N

The Peter's Railway Series

The miniature steam railway across the farm has provided plenty of adventures for Peter, Harry, Kitty, and Grandpa too. There have been school visits, construction projects, run-away grandmothers and even a bank robbery!

When Grandpa tells his amazing-but-true stories, they really did happen. Chris Vine reads a lot of old railway history books and most of them have a tale or two of some (near) disaster or crazy incident.

In the case of Driver Bill Hoole, he kept very quiet about this particular bit of mischief. If the bosses had found out about it, he would have got into a lot of trouble...

Rain, Steam and Speed

To say that it was raining at Crossacres Farm didn't really describe the situation at all. There was a deluge, a downpour, a torrent of rain falling from the sky. The raindrops were huge and seemed to be bouncing on the ground.

It had been a lovely warm afternoon when Peter, Kitty and Harry had gone out for a run on the railway. But now Peter was driving Fiery Fox at full speed, racing to get back to the engine shed where they could take shelter.

Once under cover, they looked back outside at the weather. It was clearly going to keep raining for some time yet. "I reckon that's the end of playing trains for today," Peter announced. "I'll just put the fire out, and then we can all go indoors."

"Quick, come in," laughed Grandpa, when he saw the bedraggled children. "I'll put some more logs on the fire so you can dry out."

Once the children were sitting around the blazing fire, warming up, Grandpa remembered one of his stories from the old days on the railways.

"This is a completely true story," he began, "about an engine driver called Bill Hoole, one of the best steam engine drivers of his day."

"Now, Bill Hoole was supremely competent at his job and was always in complete control of his engine and train. But, he loved going fast!"

"In fact," continued Grandpa, "he was something of a 'speed merchant'. I think that his fireman, who had to shovel an awful lot of coal, might secretly have called him a madman!"

The other thing you need to know about Bill was that he loved playing practical jokes!

Most of his exploits and adventures were well known to railwaymen. But the story I am going to tell you was so mischievous that it was kept a complete secret for many years.

The engine he drove regularly was called Seagull – one of the A4 class, designed by Sir Nigel Gresley. Seagull was the same type as Mallard, the fastest steam locomotive in the world.

Well, one day Bill Hoole was driving Seagull, north from London, on a busy stretch of railway with four tracks. It was a rotten day, with a mixture of snow and rain driving across the line.

This didn't worry Bill, he just kept an extra careful look-out for signals in the poor visibility.

When they stopped at Hitchin station, there were two young girls, standing near the end of the platform, right next to the engine. They were passengers for the train, and Bill's fireman was leaning out of the cab, talking to them.

The girls were soaking wet from the snow storm, and were also shivering from the cold.

"Why don't you come up into my warm cab?" Bill Hoole suggested to the girls. "You can dry off in the heat from the firebox. By the time you get to your stop, you will be dry and warm as toast!"

"Thank you very much!" they said, leaping up the steps into the wonderful warmth of the cab.

"Stand there," Bill instructed, pointing to a spot beside the boiler. "You won't be in the way, and you'll get the full blast of heat from the fire."

What an adventure! The girls watched carefully as Bill moved some levers and then blew the whistle with an ear-splitting shriek!

With a few quiet wheezes, the engine shuddered and started to move – slowly at first.

Blinding light and heat were streaming out of the open firehole door. Every chuff from the chimney made the fire leap and burn even brighter.

The whole machine seemed to be a huge, living, breathing monster. It was scary but exhilarating at the same time!

Faster now, the train was gathering momentum. Thunderous noise... the smell of smoke mixed with steam and hot oil... The girls' senses were completely overloaded. They roared up the line.

After a few miles, they saw a freight train ahead of them. It was running on the line next to theirs, and they were catching it up.

Bill immediately realised that the freight train was being driven by a friend of his. They usually passed it at about the same place, and would wave to each other as they went by.

It was then that he had an idea for a bit of mischief. "You see that train up ahead?" Bill asked the girls. "The driver is a good friend of mine; would you like to play a joke on him?"

Seeing the grin on Bill's face, and realising that their adventure might get even better, the girls both nodded their agreement.

There wasn't much time, so Bill Hoole quickly told the girls what he wanted them to do.

"Right," he said to one of the young girls. "You sit yourself up here, in my seat!"

He helped her up into his small leather seat, on the left hand side of the cab. She had a wonderful view ahead; the locomotive seemed to be eating up the track as it sped onwards.

"What I'd like you to do," he explained, "is to hold onto this regulator lever with your right hand, and rest your other arm on the open window frame. Just look as if the engine belongs to you!"

Then he helped the other young girl up into the fireman's seat on the other side of the cab. "If you pull on this lever," he showed her, "you can blow the whistle."

"Keep looking straight ahead," he told them both. "Pretend you have stolen the train!"

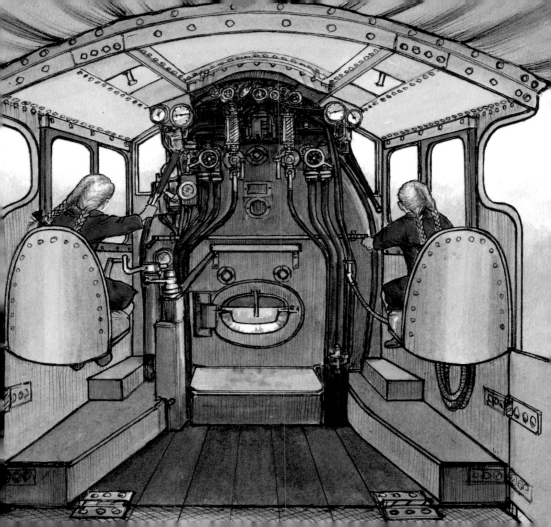

Then, to complete the illusion, the driver and fireman hid themselves out of sight. Bill tucked himself away behind one of the girls, while the fireman hid in the coal space in the tender.

"Don't worry," Bill called out. "It's quite safe, I can still see the signals ahead!"

"You two just remember to act as if the locomotive belongs to you. In fact, you can look as if you own the whole railway!"

Seagull flew on down the line, catching up with the slower freight train. Soon they were level with it, passing one wagon after another, as they caught up with the engine at the front.

The crew of the freight train saw Seagull approaching and, knowing it was their friends, they looked out of the window and waved as usual.

You can imagine their surprise when, instead of seeing Bill, there was a young girl at the regulator, and another girl blowing the whistle! With pigtails flying in the wind, and an air of complete nonchalance, they looked exactly as if they had just stolen a train!

"The look of shock on the men's faces must have been priceless," chuckled Grandpa, enjoying telling the story. "But before they could do anything, Seagull had overtaken them and was accelerating away into the distance."

"We'll never know when the men realised they had been tricked," Grandpa laughed. "But I'm sure they called Bill Hoole some very rude words!"

"Have you dried out yet?" he asked the children. "No. Please tell us another story!" they begged him.

"Well, there is one more I could tell you," smiled Grandpa. "And it's also about getting wet."

"One day, on the Great Western Railway, a very old guard, called Sam, was coupling an engine onto its train. He was standing between the tender and the first carriage, hooking on the chain."

"Unfortunately, there was a large puddle of water on the back of the tender which, when the engine moved, sloshed down all over the old man."

"The driver of the engine was Harold Gasson, and the fireman was his son, also called Harold. Well, being perfect gentlemen, they helped old Sam up into the cab, to dry out."

"Because he was soaked right through, they helped him to take off all of his clothes, right down to his underpants."

"Then they hung his wet uniform on the boiler to dry out. Trousers, jacket, shirt, hat; all dangling from the controls."

"Now Sam's underpants," explained Grandpa with a grin, "were not like any underpants you've ever seen. They were *very* old fashioned; pink, made from wool, and they covered almost his whole body. They even had a flap at the back which could be unbuttoned to perform vital functions!"

"Well, this flap was wet through," continued Grandpa. "So Sam turned his back to the fire, and stuck his bottom out to dry in the flaming heat."

"A few minutes later, he was super pleased with his warm pants. That was until..." Grandpa paused for effect, "he sat down and burned his bum. They weren't just warm, he had superheated pants!"

"Poor old Sam," smiled Grandpa. "Even that wasn't the end of his troubles. When he looked at his trusty old hat, which he had worn for at least fifty years, it had melted in the intense heat. And all the stitching had split."

"Whatever did they do?" asked the children.

"There was only one thing for it," replied Grandpa. "They threw it in the firebox. At least it wasn't wet any longer!"

"They were really good stories," laughed the children, who were now completely dry themselves.

They all agreed that they wanted to work on the railways when they were older: The great outdoors, big machines, good pay and, clearly, lots of fun too. That would be a proper job.

The End.

Why Peter's Railway?

Since a very small boy, Chris has always loved everything mechanical, especially steam engines. The first workshop was in his bedroom where he made an electric go-kart when only 8, followed by a mini-bike powered by the engine from a petrol lawn mower.

He spent many holidays on a friend's farm where there was a miniature railway across a field, and so started a love of making model steam locomotives. The latest is Bongo, 8 feet long and the inspiration for Fiery Fox in the books.

Chris wanted to share his love and knowledge of railways and engineering: Peter's Railway is the result.

Books for children who love trains and engineering

Story

Pistons and Cylinders
How the steam turns the wheels and drives the locomotive

Technical

History

Adventure

The hardback books

The five hardback books tell the charming story of Peter and his Grandpa building and running their steam railway across the farm. At the ends of chapters are special how-it-works pages with simple (but accurate) explanations of what has been happening in the story. In addition, Grandpa tells some wonderful stories from the old days on the railways.   Age range 6 - 12 years approx.

A new steam railway is born.

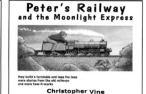

Points, turntables and Peter drives Fiery Fox.

The line is extended and The Great Railway Race.

They build a watermill to power the farm.

Peter helps save the world and makes lots of money!

Activity book with puzzles and colouring - paperback.

Hardback, 96 pages 17 x 24 cm with 30 watercolour pictures by John Wardle and 14 pages of clearly explained technical drawings. £11.99

Paperback books

A series of Peter's Railway in a smaller format. While the original books each contain several story or adventure threads, separate technical pages and Grandpa's tales, the small books concentrate on one aspect; an adventure, a tale from the old railways or a technical book. The four *Little* books are for younger readers.

An adventure on a Scottish holiday which ends with a bang!
Age 6 to 12 years

A true story about an unlucky engine and a brave fireman.
Age 6 to 12 years

A crazy mistake leads to disaster. One of Grandpa's true stories.
Age 6 to 12 years

A cab-ride in a modern diesel and a story from the old days.
Age 6 to 12 years

Our two heroes build a new locomotive from scrap.
Age 6 to 12 years

Grandpa tries to answer a tricky question.
Age 6 to 12 years

The children foil a plot and cause destruction!
Age 6 to 12 years

A storm, getting wet and stealing a train!
Age 6 to 12 years

Peter saves Christmas, a gentle tale.

A bed-time story with a twist...

A railway picnic soon turns into mayhem...

Playing trains on an epic scale!

Little Peter's Railway - Four gentle tales for younger readers, age 3 to 6 years